POCAHONTAS

POCAHONTAS
The True Story of an American Hero and Her Christian Faith

Text by Andy Holmes
Illustrations by Jim Conaway

 Published in the United States by Little Moorings, a division of the Balantine Publishing Group, Random House Inc., New York, and simultaneously in Canada by Random House of Canada Limited, Toronto.

ISBN: 0-345-40361-4

Library of Congress Catalog Card Number: 95-79435

Manufactured in the United States of America

First Edition: September 1995
1 3 5 7 9 8 6 4 2

The True Story of an American Hero and Her Christian Faith

ANDY HOLMES

Illustrated by Jim Conaway

"Look, Nakoo." The Indian princess pointed at the colorful sky. "Isn't it beautiful? Watch. Soon we will see the sun."

Pocahontas snatched Nakoo up in her hands and plopped the spotted salamander down beside her.

"How does the sun know when to come up?" She stroked Nakoo's forehead. "Someone must tell it to. A god? A god of many colors."

Nakoo twisted over onto his back hoping to have his belly scratched. The little princess giggled. "My father is right, Nakoo. You are a silly pet." She scrubbed his tummy playfully then scooted him off the rock onto the dew-drenched grass.

"I'll be a woman soon, Nakoo." Pocahontas jumped to a higher rock. "Who will watch the sky with you once my days are filled with important tasks?" Deep in her heart she knew she would be a part of something very special. "I am the favorite daughter of the great King Powhatan. I will work hard to make him proud."

The sunlight blinded Nakoo's drowsy eyes. He buried his dotted face under the edge of a moss-covered stone and let his tail flop in the sunshine.

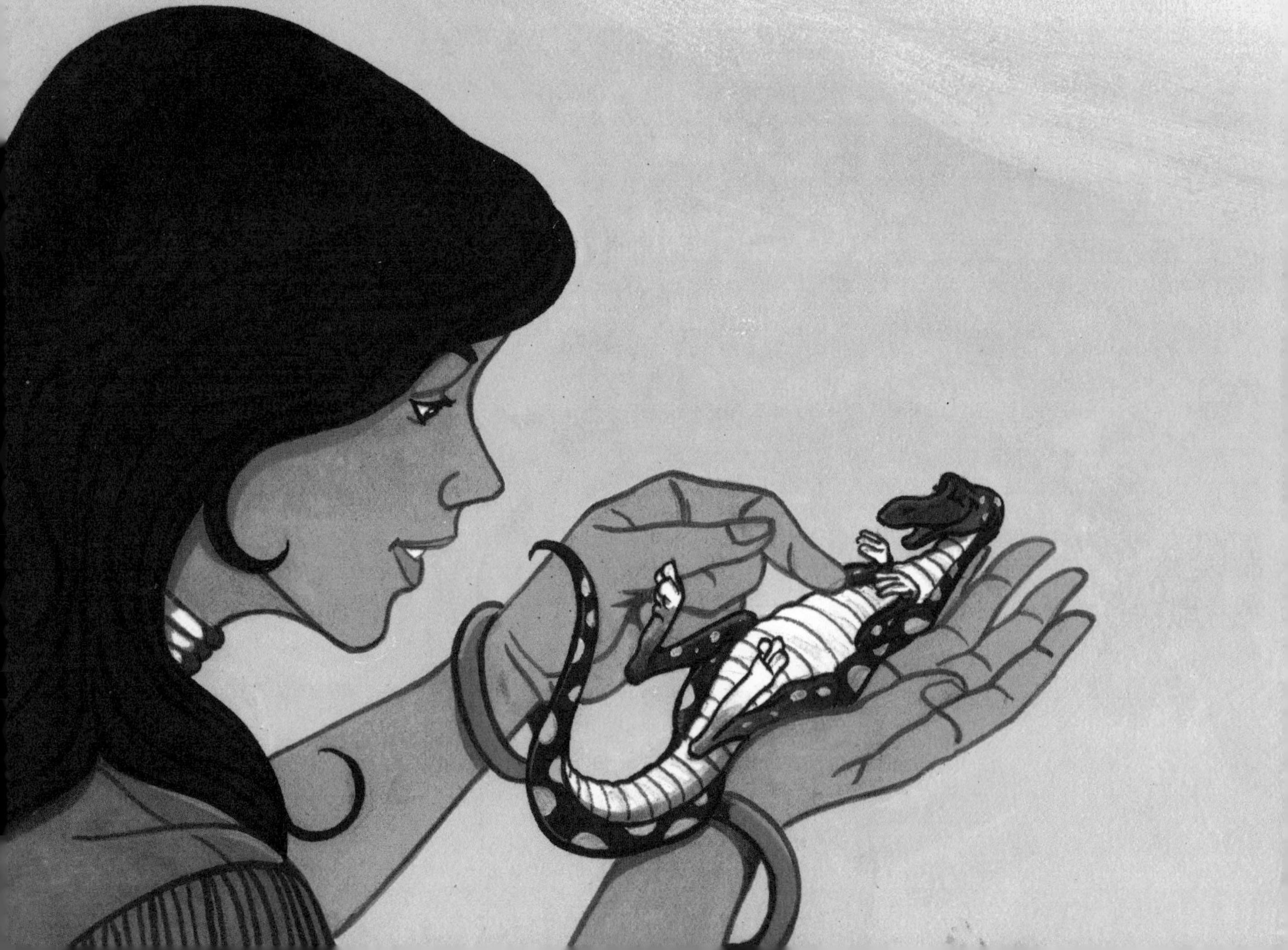

"They're here! They're here!" a young brave screamed as he rushed past Pocahontas. She leaped off the tall rock and raced after him. "*Who's* here, Swift-of-Foot?"

"The white demons!" Swift-of-Foot snarled.

Pocahontas had always been curious about the mysterious, pale-faced strangers she'd heard tales about. Glancing up at the sky she wondered if the God who filled the air with colors knew of the white-skinned people as well.

Pocahontas arrived and found the whole village astir with excitement. All whispers hushed as the tall, commanding Chief Powhatan rose to his feet.

"The white demons have returned. Again, we will drive them into the sea with our mighty bows and our sharp arrows."

Everyone danced and cheered. But not Pocahontas. She couldn't stop wondering, *Maybe the white man comes in peace.*

"Land ho! Land ho!"

The discouraged voyagers rubbed their eyes. After almost five months at sea had they finally found their Virginia?

Captain John Smith gripped the rail of the *Susan Constant* as the sea-battered ship pulled into the quiet cove.

This is it, Smith secretly determined. *This is my new home.*

Two of Powhatan's sharpest scouts spied on John Smith as he explored the land. Suddenly, a large wildcat stepped into the grassy patch, not more than thirty feet from the captain.

Eyes-like-Eagle and Bear-Heart froze. *This is a sign,* Eyes-like-Eagle reasoned. *Our god Okeus has sent a wildcat to destroy the white men for us and to chase them from our land.*

The fierce cat crouched low, never taking its eyes off its prey, then suddenly lunged at the captain. John Smith steadied his gun.

"Boom!"

The two braves grabbed their ears and fell to the ground. Smoke billowed from the white man's strange stick.

"Look!" Eyes-like-Eagle pointed just beyond the white man where the wild beast lay dead. "We must tell Powhatan!"

Pocahontas had never seen Eyes-like-Eagle and Bear-Heart so excited as she watched them give her father their report of the white man's camp. "They bind themselves in heavy clothing and grow hair on their faces."

Bear-Heart interrupted, "They speak with strange words."

"And they have canoes as big as mountains!" Eyes-like-Eagle added, stretching his arms wide.

Powhatan showed no emotion. "Tell me of their weapons."

"We saw no swords, bows, or spears, Great King," Eyes-like-Eagle explained, his ears still ringing, "but when the white man pointed a glowing stick at a wildcat, it boomed! The beast was dead."

The whole village gasped.

"Come." The great chief lead the braves to the meeting hall. "We must plan our attack."

Pocahontas cradled Nakoo on her arm. "What's wrong with me, Nakoo? Why don't I fear the white men, too?" The little princess stared into the star-filled sky and sighed. "I must see them for myself, Nakoo. With my own eyes. Or my heart will never rest." Pocahontas lay Nakoo down in a patch of moist leaves, unsure if she'd ever see her tiny friend again. "I will leave before the next sun rises."

The morning sun beat down on the colonists' camp. Many were starving and John Smith knew he would have to leave the camp and find some willing tribes who could trade goods and food. If not, they all would die.

John Smith trudged through the darkened forest, his legs shaking with fatigue. He collapsed beside a cool stream and soon fell into a deep sleep.

Soft flickers of moonlight provided Pocahontas with her first view of the white man. *He's so different from our braves,* she thought. *A man, yes, but very pale.*

Slowly, she reached to feel his heavy wool jacket. John Smith awoke and grabbed Pocahontas by the shoulders and wrestled her to the ground. He raised a stone high above his head then threw it aside.

"You're just a child!" he gasped. "A girl!"

Pocahontas's heart raced. Though she couldn't understand his strange words, she sensed he would not hurt her. She nodded her head and timidly smiled at the nervous stranger. John Smith smiled back and sighed.

"My name is J-ooarrggghh!" cried Smith, his right arm suddenly throbbing from the sting of an arrow. The wounded captain quickly rolled into the thicket but soon blacked out.

John Smith woke to the beating of drums. His mind felt sluggish and his vision blurred. Just then, two muscular men yanked him to his feet and dragged him to their warrior-chief. Their king glared at the injured captain and gave a slight nod to the two braves.

Before he could blink, John Smith was forced to his knees and his head shoved against a flat, cold stone. *God in Heaven*, Smith prayed behind tight lips, *I'm a man of many mistakes. I don't deserve your mercy, but I beg you. Please don't let me die! Please.*

A third brave solemnly approached the rock, lifted his tomahawk high awaiting his chief's command. John Smith clenched his teeth, and squeezed his eyes shut.

The huge executioner heaved his richly painted chest and raised his hammer to strike.

"Shaaaaaaaaaaaaaaaaaaaaaaaaaaaaaaaaaaaaaaaaa!"

Smith's body jerked at the sudden and piercing scream. He felt warm arms wrap around the back of his neck. Looking up, he saw a young girl, his little friend from the woods, kneeling in front of him.

"Please, Father, please!" she said to Chief Powhatan. "He means us no harm! Let him live!" she cried.

The captain was released and given a place to live among them. Pocahontas visited him every day and quickly learned the white man's language and of Smith's hungry companions.

"Father?" The wise chief gestured for her to sit down. "The white men need food," she continued. "They are starving." Powhatan looked away. "Perhaps we can trade with them," she prodded, "for their magic sticks."

The great king raised an eyebrow. “Well done, Little Mischief,” Powhatan teased. He knew she preferred other nicknames but wanted to make her aware that her kindness to the white men might lead to trouble. “I will give them food.”

Pocahontas loved the pale-faced people. She asked their preacher, the Reverend Whitaker, many questions about God. He told her the story of God creating the sky, sun, and earth.

Pocahontas noticed how the parson's eyes sparkled when he would tell her how much the one true God loved her. Her big, brown eyes filled with tears when she learned how God had sent his only Son to die so that all people could live in true and everlasting peace.

"You see, Princess," the Reverend Whitaker explained, "God loves all men the same."

"Are you all right, Princess?" She felt the preacher's hand on her arm. Pocahontas smiled, then nodded at her caring friend.

Pocahontas spent much of her time helping secure food and supplies so that the struggling colony could not only survive, but prosper.

More and more people left England to build a new life for themselves in the new land, but one in particular caught the interest of the maturing Pocahontas. His name was John Rolfe.

Pocahontas loved to sit and listen to him read stories from the Bible. "Even though I am just now learning about him, John," Pocahontas shared, "I feel like I have known Jesus all my life."

"Yes, and now you know his name." He squeezed her tight. She had never felt happier.

Slowly their love for one another grew as well. They took walks through the woods together, watched sunrises together, shared meals together.

One day, Pocahontas had some very important news to share. "I've been praying a lot, John, and I've decided to be baptized just like the others were in the Bible." John Rolfe swooped her up in his arms and spun around and around. "That's wonderful, Pocahontas! Absolutely wonderful!"

John Rolfe smiled as Pocahontas waded into the water and was joined by the Reverend Whitaker. "Do you believe that Jesus Christ is the Son of God?"

Pocahontas nodded. "Yes. Yes, I do."

"And do you desire to serve him with all your heart, soul, strength, and mind?"

"Yes, very much," the princess answered.

"Then I now baptize you in the name of the Father, Son, and Holy Spirit for the forgiveness of every sin, every mistake."

Pocahontas cupped her hands over her nose and mouth as the Reverend Whitaker lowered her into the water, then raised her back up. "Today you have become brand-new," the pastor explained as he reached to hug her tight. "Welcome, sister," he whispered.

Within a year, John Rolfe and Pocahontas were married. The happy newlyweds left the flower-filled chapel as the evening sun disappeared behind the dark, green forest. Pocahontas looked around at the crowd of friends—pale-faced and copper-skinned.

Surely, she reasoned, *this marriage of two nations holds a promise of blessing.*

"Look, Princess!" It was the Reverend Whitaker's little boy, Nathaniel. "I found him under the steps!" Pocahontas gazed at the black salamander whose bright yellow spots seemed to almost glow. *Nakoo!* The new bride whispered to herself. *Look what's happened. Now our land is like you. Sharing two colors.*

Pocahontas stared reflectively at the soothing colors of the setting sun and smiled. She finally understood why her desire for peace had been so deep. It was the work of the ultimate Peacemaker, the bidding of the one true God.

Her handsome new husband gently squeezed her hand, then lovingly lifted her into the waiting carriage. Pocahontas was happy and her heart was full.